This book belongs to

_____

_____

ORCHARD BOOKS

First published in the United States in 2020 by Little, Brown and Company
First published in Great Britain in 2021 by The Watts Publishing Group

Text copyright © 2020 by Tom Rosenthal
Illustrations copyright © 2020 by Hannah Jacobs

ISBN: 978-1-40836-506-9

1 3 5 7 9 10 8 6 4 2

Printed and bound in China

FSC
www.fsc.org

MIX
Paper from
responsible sources
FSC® C104740

Orchard Books
An imprint of Hachette Children's Group
Part of The Watts Publishing Group Limited

Carmelite House, 50 Victoria Embankment, London EC4Y 0DZ

An Hachette UK Company
www.hachette.co.uk   www.hachettechildrens.co.uk

DINOSAURS IN ♥VE

Fenn Rosenthal

Illustrations by **Hannah Jacobs**

ORCHARD

Dinosaurs eating people.

Dinosaurs in love.

Dinosaurs having a party.

They eat fruit . . .

and cucumber.

They fell in love.

They say, "Thank you."

A
BIG BANG
came.

And they died.

Dinosaurs,

dinosaurs . . .

Fell in love.

But they didn't
say goodbye.

But they didn't say goodbye.

A Letter from Fenn's Dad (Tom Rosenthal)

I couldn't begin to tell you why she had three hard-boiled eggs for lunch that day. Nearly-four-year-olds are truly *wild* beasts. But half an hour later, she bounced into my home studio, asking if we could "do a song".

Fast-forward a couple of days. It felt like I had spoken to half the world's journalists. What a strange world we live in where a few afternoon moments in a quiet London room can be beamed round the world within hours of their happening. Now, some months on, and with the release of this beautiful book (kudos to the wondrous illustrator, Hannah!), I asked Fenn, now four and a half, a few questions about what it feels like to have her words become print!

Me: What are you most excited about for when your book comes out?
Fenn: When I go to the library, I'll read my own book. I'll say, "My book is called *Dinosaurs In Love*," and the shopkeeper (librarian) will say, "How do you know that name?"

Me: How will it feel if lots of people read your book?
Fenn: It kind of makes me feel that I'm a bit famous, but I'm not, actually.

Me: How many people do you think will read your book?
Fenn: One hundred! *looks very proud of herself*

© Tom Rosenthal, 2020

© Emma Jacobs, 2020

Fenn Rosenthal was born in 2016 and wrote *Dinosaurs In Love* when she was just three years old. In 2020, Fenn and her sister, Bess, released an EP of their songs titled *They're Awake!* Fenn lives in London with her family.

Hannah Jacobs is a director, animator, and illustrator from London. Her films have screened worldwide at festivals including official selection for SXSW, Tribeca, Annecy Festival, LIAF, MONSTRA, and Rooftop Films. This is her first picture book.